First published 1987 by
Walker Books Ltd
184-192 Drummond Street
London NW1 3HP

Text and illustrations © 1987 Myriad Productions Ltd

Back cover photograph by Alistair Morrison

First printed 1987
Printed and bound by L.E.G.O., Vicenza, Italy

British Library Cataloguing in Publication Data
Asher, Jane
Moppy is happy.
I. Title II. Scarfe, Gerald
823′.914[J]   PZ7

ISBN 0-7445-0765-0
ISBN 0-7445-0783-9 Pbk

MOPPY IS HAPPY

Written by
JANE ASHER

Illustrated by
GERALD SCARFE

WALKER BOOKS
LONDON

David was lying in bed one evening
thinking. It had been a terrible day.
His mum and dad had been busy and
his friends never wanted to come over
and play with him. Life was really boring
and now he couldn't go to sleep.

Then, as he lay watching the shadows
on the ceiling, he heard a strange
whizzing noise, and he thought he saw
something bright green flash
down past his window.

"Am I dreaming?" David wondered.

He put one foot out of bed and onto the floor. It felt very cold.

"Well, I'm certainly awake," he said out loud. "And I'm going to go outside and find out what that was."

It was very dark outside and David felt a bit scared.

He was sure he had seen something
but there wasn't anything

on the swing

or behind the tree

or in the old flower-pot.

Then he heard a rustling noise coming
from the watering can. He plucked up
courage.

"Who's there?" he shouted bravely.

"Nobody," answered a squeaky voice.

David thought for a moment. "You must
be somebody or you couldn't talk," he said.

Then he saw something green leap out of the
can and disappear behind the bushes.
"Where have you gone?" asked David.
"Nowhere," answered the squeaky voice.
"You must be somewhere," said David.
"Why don't you come out?"

The green thing darted out and leapt at the washing line.

"Who are you?" said David.

"Can't you see?" it answered. "I'm a shirt."

"No you're not. Don't be so silly," said David, who was getting a bit cross by now. "Come down here and tell me who you really are."

The green creature let go of the washing line and landed at David's feet.

"My name is Moppy," it said. "I jumped down from a star very high up in space. I don't know what to do now."

"Perhaps you'd like to come to stay with me for a bit," said David. "You don't bite or anything, do you?"

"Only food," answered Moppy. "And I'd love to stay. You seem very friendly."

David looked worried. "The only trouble is, I'm not sure how Mum and Dad will feel about it. Perhaps I'd better hide you."

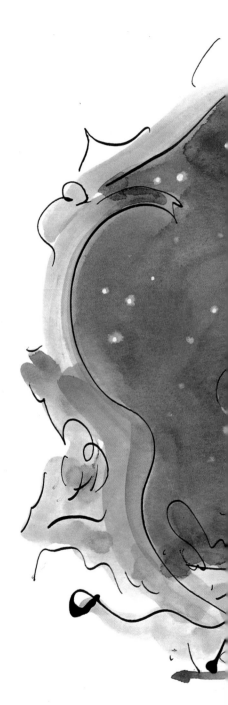

Moppy and David walked across the garden towards the house.

"Did you really jump all the way from space?" asked David.

"Oh yes," said Moppy. "I often do that."

They peeped in at the sitting-room window.

"Look," said Moppy. "There are two funny people in there looking at a square box."

"That's Mum and Dad watching television, stupid," whispered David. "Come on!"

David and Moppy crept into the house, quietly shutting the door behind them, and started to go upstairs.

At that moment David's father came out of the sitting-room. David and Moppy ran to hide behind the grandfather clock.

"Who's there?" said Mr Jones.

"NOBODY!" shouted Moppy and David together, and then they both started to giggle.

"Come on, David, I know it's you," said Mr Jones. "What are you doing out of bed and which of your friends is with you?"

David came out from behind the clock.

"Come on, Moppy," he said. "It's no use hiding any longer."

Moppy crept slowly out.

"What on earth is that?" shrieked Mrs Jones, who was watching from the sitting-room doorway.

"He's a green creature who jumped from space and he's my friend," said David. "Oh please, please let him stay here," he begged.

"I'll look after him. He won't be any trouble."

"Oh yes, David,"
said Mrs Jones. "Just like you
take care of the goldfish,
I suppose. Just look at
his dirty tank."

"It's all right, Mrs Jones,"
said Moppy. "I can look after
myself. And as a matter of
fact I'm also rather good at
cleaning out goldfish."

"Perhaps you can stay then,"
laughed Mrs Jones. "You
might even help keep David
clean too. He always seems
to be covered in mud.
Yes, you can stay and sleep
in David's room."

Suddenly something very strange happened.

Moppy's toes turned yellow.

The next moment
his arms did too,

then his legs,

and then his tummy and face until he was
completely yellow all over.

"How extraordinary!" said Mrs Jones.

"It's because I'm happy," said Moppy.

"Sometimes I change colour when I feel things."

"I'm happy too," said David, and he looked down to see whether his toes had turned yellow, but they hadn't. He smiled at his mum and dad, then turned and picked up the bright yellow Moppy.

Halfway up the stairs he stopped, and whispered in Moppy's ear, "I'll be your best friend if you like. I wonder what colour you'll turn tomorrow."

"I wonder," thought Moppy, as David
tucked him under his arm and took him
upstairs to bed.